# Goldsworthy and Mort
## in
## Holiday Hijinks

# Goldsworthy and Mort

in

## Holiday Hijinks

by Marcia Vaughan

pictures by Linda Hendry

A Ready ☆ Set ☆ Read® Book

HarperCollins*PublishersLtd*

For Sam,
who knows how to have fun
M.V.

For Shel
L.H.

**Produced by Caterpillar Press**

Ready ☆ Set ☆ Read is a registered trademark of
HarperCollins Publishers Ltd

**Canadian Cataloguing in Publication Data**

Vaughan, Marcia K.
    Goldsworthy & Mort in holiday hijinks

"A ready set read book".
ISBN 0-00-647505-1

I. Hendry, Linda.  II. Title.

PZ7.V38Go 1993    j823    C93-094617-0

# Contents

# Christmas Gift Catastrophe

Christmas was coming.

The air was cold as ice.

Christmas trees twinkled

in windows, splashing bright

lights across the snow.

Goldsworthy and Mort were

busy getting ready.

"Deck the halls with boughs
of holly," sang Goldsworthy
as he decorated his tree,
hung up his stocking and
sent cards to all his friends.

"Jingle bells, jingle bells,

jingle all the way," sang Mort

as he wrapped presents,

hung up mistletoe and put a

big round wreath on his door.

"I have only one thing left to do,"

hummed Goldsworthy,

checking his 'to do' list.

"And that is buy Mort

a present. A very special

best-friend sort of present.

A present Mort will really love."

Goldsworthy grabbed his gloves

and galoshes and hurried in to town.

Meanwhile, Mort was checking

his 'don't forget' list.

"I have only one thing

left to do," he smiled.

"And that is buy Goldsworthy

a gift. A very special

best-buddy kind of gift.

A gift Goldsworthy will really love."

Mort threw on his muffler and

mittens and hurried off to town.

"I wonder what Mort

wants for Christmas,"

Goldsworthy pondered

as he peered in windows.

"I wonder what Goldsworthy

wants for Christmas,"

Mort murmured as he wandered

up and down aisles.

Goldsworthy looked at

colored can openers,

slippery slippers and tacky ties.

"I don't see anything that is

right for Mort," he grumbled.

Mort looked at dumbbells,

schoolbells and ugly undies.

"I don't see anything that is

right for Goldsworthy,"

Mort mumbled.

"And tomorrow is Christmas."

Goldsworthy tramped home.

Mort stamped home.

Neither one had found a gift.

Goldsworthy soaked in

a bubbly tub, thinking.

"I know!" he cried,

blowing bubbles around the room.

"If I cannot buy Mort a present

I will *make* him one.

I will build him a

spin-around footstool with

an automatic up and down device.

That is exactly what Mort needs to

rest his feet by the fire.

He will love it!"

Meanwhile, Mort was marching

around his tree, thinking.

"I know!" he cried.

"If I cannot buy Goldsworthy a gift

I will *make* him one.

I will knit him an

extra-special snowsuit sweater.

That is just what Goldsworthy

needs to stay warm when

we play in the snow.

He will love it!"

Goldsworthy rummaged around in his basement.

He took out a hammer, saw, springs and all sorts of building things.

Mort poked around in his attic.

He found two chopsticks and a pile

of old, worn out sweaters to unravel.

*Wham, clank, boink, bang*

went Goldsworthy as he

built Mort's present.

*Click, clack, clicketty clack*

went Mort as he

knitted Goldsworthy's gift.

"This is going to be the most

perfect present Mort could

ever wish for,"

Goldsworthy smiled as he

hammered away.

"This is going to be the best gift

Goldsworthy ever got!"

grinned Mort as he knitted.

*Bang. Boink. Clang.*

Goldsworthy worked all night.

He worked until all the wood

and springs and building things

were used up.

Goldsworthy stood back and

looked at the footstool.

He looked at the sizeable seat.

He looked at the high base.

He looked at the big springs.

"I'm not so sure this footstool

is the right size for Mort's feet,"

he worried.

"But it is too late to

buy another present.

Oh, sour sugar plums,"

Goldsworthy grumbled.

"Now I don't have a Christmas

present for my very best friend."

*Click. Clicketty. Clack.*

Mort knit and knit and

knit all night, until

the yarn was all used up.

He held up the snowsuit sweater.

He looked at the three legs.

He looked at the two necks.

He looked at the one long arm.

"I'm not so sure this is

going to fit Goldsworthy,"

he worried.

"But it is too late

to get another gift.

Oh, crumbled candy canes,"

Mort moped.

"Now I don't have a Christmas

gift for my best buddy."

Early the next morning

Mort woke up.

With a sad sigh, he wrapped the

snowsuit sweater in red paper

and tramped through

the silvery snow

to Goldsworthy's house.

Goldsworthy was already up.

He had just finished wrapping the

footstool in white tissue paper.

"Merry Christmas, Goldsworthy.

Here is a gift," said Mort sadly.

"For me?" said Goldsworthy.

He forgot all about the footstool.

"Here is a present for you, too,"

Goldsworthy added.

"Goody!" cried Mort,

forgetting all about

the snowsuit sweater.

Goldsworthy ripped off the
red wrapping.

Mort tore off the white tissue.

Goldsworthy held up his gift
and gasped.

"It's marvelous, Mort.

It is *just* what I wanted.

I love it!"

Mort looked mixed up.

"You wanted a snowsuit sweater with three legs, two necks and one long arm?"

"No," giggled Goldsworthy.

"I wanted new warm winter woollies for my scarecrow. How clever of you to knit it to fit!"

A smile spread across Mort's face.

"I'm glad you like it, Goldsworthy."

Mort marched around his

present with surprise.

"And this present is perfect, too.

It is *exactly* what I wanted.

I love it!"

Goldsworthy looked confused.

"You wanted a too-big spin-around footstool with an automatic up and down device?"

"No," laughed Mort.

"I wanted a super-duper snowball shooter with catapult power just like this."

A grin spread across Goldsworthy's face.

"I'm glad you like it, Mort."

Mort gave Goldsworthy a
big, happy holiday hug.
"Merry Christmas, best buddy
of mine," he said.

Goldsworthy hugged Mort
right back.
"Merry Christmas to you, too,
best friend."

Then Goldsworthy grabbed his

gloves and galoshes.

Mort threw on his

mittens and muffler.

Together they dressed the scarecrow

in its new winter woollies.

Then they loaded the

snowball shooter.

Whoosh. Shoosh. Splat!

Goldsworthy and Mort

ran and laughed

and dodged snowballs all afternoon.

They were two best friends,

happy to be together

on Christmas day.

On Vacation

Goldsworthy was sitting by

the fire looking grumpy.

Mort marched into his house.

He sank into a chair.

"Mort, I am tired of sitting

by the same old fire,"

grumbled Goldsworthy.

"Goldsworthy, I am tired of

walking in the same old woods,"

mumbled Mort.

"All we ever eat is soup, soup, soup," griped Goldsworthy.

"All we ever see are the same old places, day after day," moped Mort.

Goldsworthy stared at the flickering flames of fire.

"Do you know what we are, Mort?" he sighed.

"What, Goldsworthy?" asked Mort.

"We are bored."

"Uh-oh," murmured Mort.

"That sounds bad. What do we do to get rid of it?"

Goldsworthy twitched his whiskers.

He drummed his paws on the table.

Suddenly, he leaped to his feet.

"What we must do, Mort,"

he began, "is go on vacation.

We must travel to new and

exciting places.

We must eat foreign food.

We must see all sorts of

sensational sights."

Mort jumped up.

"Goody gumballs, Goldsworthy!"

he cried.

"When can we go?"

"As soon as we pack our bags,"

answered Goldsworthy.

Goldsworthy packed a warm jacket,
woolly socks and sensible shoes
in his suitcase.

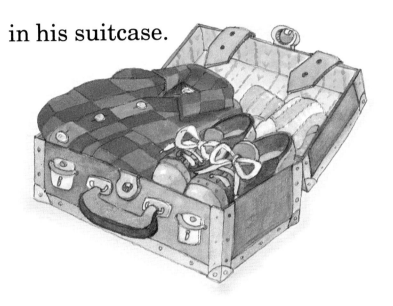

Mort stuffed sunglasses,
swim trunks and sandals
into his backpack.

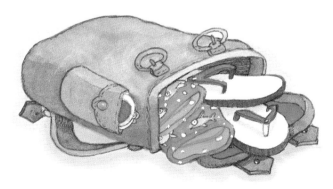

"Where shall we go first?"

wondered Mort.

Goldsworthy studied his map.

"I've always wanted to

climb a mountain," he said.

"Let's go to Switzerland."

Goldsworthy and Mort trekked

to the tip-most, top-most peak

of the tallest mountain.

"I feel like I'm on top of the world,"

said Goldsworthy.

"Brrr. This place is too cold for me,"

shivered Mort. "I feel like an icicle.

Let's go somewhere sunny.

Let's go to Australia."

Goldsworthy and Mort went surfing,

sailing, snorkeling and sunbathing.

"I feel so fit and fine,"

marveled Mort,

admiring his tan muscles.

"Phew," said Goldsworthy,

unzipping his jacket.

"I feel as hot as melted butter.

Let's go somewhere and

see the sights."

In London, Goldsworthy and Mort whizzed around town on double-decker buses.

They saw old castles, old bridges and old statues.

"Blimey," bristled Goldsworthy.

"This place is too crowded

for me. Let's go somewhere

with fewer people.

Let's go to Egypt."

In Egypt, Goldsworthy and Mort

cantered on camels,

played on pyramids

and tip-toed through tombs.

"Swirling sand storms,"

coughed Mort.

"This place is too dry for me.

I feel like a dustball.

Let's go somewhere with water.

Let's go to Italy."

In Italy, Goldsworthy and Mort rented a long black gondola. They poled up and down the canals. Other gondolas with motors whizzed past, whooshing waves over the two travelers.

"Help!" gurgled Goldsworthy,

clinging to the side.

"This place is too wet for me.

I feel like a flounder.

Let's go somewhere exciting.

Let's go to Spain."

In Spain, Goldsworthy and Mort played guitars, danced the flamenco and met some bulls.

"Run!" cried Mort.

"Faster!" cried Goldsworthy.

They raced down the narrow streets,

across the square,

around the fountain

and up the steps to their hotel.

Goldsworthy collapsed on the couch.

Mort toppled onto the bed.

"Gosh, Goldsworthy," panted Mort,

"this place is a little too

exciting for me."

Goldsworthy nodded.

"This place is a *lot* too exciting

for me," he said.

Mort sighed.

"Where shall we go next,

Goldsworthy?

The North Pole? The South Pole?

The Amazon?"

Goldsworthy slipped off

his sensible shoes.

He looked at the holes in the soles.

"My feet are aching," he admitted.

"I am too tuckered out to

tour another town."

Mort yawned.

"And I am too exhausted to see another sensational sight."

"Mort," said Goldsworthy, rubbing his tender toes.

"Do you know what we are?"

"What, Goldsworthy?" said Mort.

"We are not bored anymore," Goldsworthy said.

"We are ready to go home."

"Really, Goldsworthy?

Are you sure?" asked Mort.

"Absolutely," Goldsworthy nodded.

"Goody gumballs, Goldsworthy!

When can we go?" cried Mort,

jumping off the bed.

"As soon as we pack our bags,"

answered Goldsworthy.

Goldsworthy folded his clothes and

quickly put them in his suitcase.

Mort stuffed his souvenirs

and swim gear into his backpack.

They zoomed straight home.

Goldsworthy was sitting by
the fire looking pleased.
Mort strolled into his house
carrying a pot of soup.
"How fine it is to sit by
the fire," grinned Goldsworthy,
wiggling his toasty toes.
"How wonderful it is to
walk in the woods," smiled Mort,
stirring the soup.
"This place is the *best* place
in the whole wide world,"
said Goldsworthy.

"This place is the *best* place

to be," agreed Mort.

The two friends sat by the fire

sipping soup and singing songs,

happy to be home again.